HORSE STORIES

by
ROBIN JONSON

kidsbooks
Incorporated

KIDSBOOKS, INCORPORATED
7004 N. CALIFORNIA AVE.
CHICAGO, IL 60645
U.S.A.

ISBN 0-942025-18-0

COVER PHOTO ANIMALS/ANIMALS ROBERT MAIER
MANUFACTURED IN THE UNITED STATES OF AMERICA

Contents

Lady

Carolyn pushed her nose against the car window. Rain splattered the glass and it was hard to see out. Blurred shapes whizzed by on the highway.

"Can I ride even if it's raining, Dad?" Carolyn asked.

Ed Jordan didn't take his eyes off the rain-slicked highway. The wipers cleared away the streaks on the windshield, but the drops were big and heavy. The gray sky meant this was more than a passing shower. "We'll see how it looks when we get to the stable," he answered. He knew how much his daughter looked forward to riding her horse every Saturday morning.

But Ed Jordan was a cautious man. He would not take chances on the highway. He would not let his daughter take chances on a slippery riding trail.

Carolyn's face turned to a frown. "That means 'no,' " she said. She scrunched down in her seat and stared straight ahead.

Her dad patted her on the knee. "I said we'll see when we get there," he said with a smile. "If Harry Carlson says the trail is safe, you can ride."

The frown on Carolyn's face melted just a little. Harry Carlson, the man who owned Green Gable Stable, was her friend. He had helped her pick Lady for her very own. That was over a year ago, on her birthday. "Lady's the best of the lot," he said then. "She still is," Carolyn said aloud.

"What did you say?" Mr. Jordan asked.

Carolyn smiled. "I was just thinking about when you bought Lady for me," she said. "Mr. Carlson said she was the best of the lot and she still is."

Mr. Jordan turned off the main highway.

The road to the stable was a narrow country lane. It was barely wide enough for two cars. "I think she's the best of the lot, too," he said. He turned his attention back to driving.

Carolyn was an excellent rider. Her grandfather had said so when he put her on a pony for the first time. Carolyn was only three years old. The pony was named Clyde. Carolyn knew then that horses would be her favorite animal. Some of her friends liked dogs. Others liked cats. And one, MaryBeth Holliday, had a goat. But Carolyn loved horses. Especially one horse—Lady.

"I wonder if Lady misses me as much as I miss her?" Carolyn asked.

"I'm sure she does," Mr. Jordan answered. He slowed down to make room for a pickup truck coming from the opposite direction. "Say, isn't that the pickup from the stable?"

Carolyn squirmed around in her seat. The truck passed too quickly to see clearly. "It's too rainy to tell," she said.

"He was driving awfully fast for this narrow road," Mr. Jordan said.

A shiver made Carolyn sit up straight. Her blue eyes opened wide. "Something is wrong at the stable," she said in a voice so quiet it was almost lost.

Ed Jordan turned to his daughter. This kind of thing had happened before. There were times when Carolyn could sense trouble. "We'll be there in five minutes," he said. "I'm sure everything is just fine."

The rest of the ride was quiet. Mr. Jordan didn't want to upset his daughter. But Carolyn was already upset. Something terrible had happened at the stable, she was certain.

Harry Carlson stood just inside the large stable door as the Jordan car entered the drive. He waved. He was a big man with a big smile and hands as large as skillets. A bright yellow rain jacket covered his broad back. And of course he wore cowboy boots. "Pull on inside," he shouted to Ed

Jordan. "No point getting soaked if you don't have to." He stepped aside so the car could enter the barn.

"Is Lady all right?" Carolyn shouted as she leaped out of the car.

Harry Carlson tipped his hat back with his hand. "Now what kind of a question is that?" he asked. "Of course she's all right." He straightened his hat. "Take a look if you don't believe me."

But Carolyn had already run by Mr. Carlson. She dashed past stall after stall. She knew all of the horses by name. But on this Saturday morning she was only interested in one. "Lady!" she called.

An answering whinny sounded from the stall at the very end of the long barn. Carolyn let out a giant sigh of relief. "Oh, Lady," she gasped. "You're all right."

Carolyn quickly unbolted the stall door. She slipped inside. Her horse, a chestnut-colored mare, with a bright star on her chest, tossed her head up and down. "Did you miss me?" Carolyn asked happily.

9

Lady tossed her head again.

Without being told, Carolyn began her weekly chores. A pitchfork with a handle cut down to her size leaned against the stall rail. "I'll clean your stall first," she said as she reached for the pitchfork. "Then I'll get you some nice, fresh straw and a..."

"Screeeeech! Fwoooommp!"

A shrill screech followed by a thunderous crash echoed through the open barn door. Carolyn whirled around.

Harry Carlson was racing out the door. Carolyn's father was right behind him. The rain was coming down in buckets. Carolyn couldn't see why they were running. She dropped the pitchfork and ran to the door.

An orange glow filled the air. Something was burning fiercely down the road. Carolyn shielded her eyes from the rain. It was just over the hill and out of sight. Her father and Mr. Carlson were running toward the glow.

"What on earth was that?"

Midge Sawyer, Harry Carlson's stable

manager, burst from her office door. She joined Carolyn at the open barn door.

"I don't know," Carolyn said. "I was back there." She turned briefly toward the row of stalls behind her. Then she looked back at the road. Her father and Mr. Carlson had vanished over the top of the hill.

Midge cupped her hands to her mouth. Her eyes were wide with fear. "I sent Perry to town for supplies," she said. "He took the pickup...."

Carolyn knew at once what Midge was thinking. The rain-slicked narrow road. The speeding pickup truck. She put her hand in Midge's.

"It sounded like a crash," Midge said. "But maybe it was just..."

Suddenly the sky lit up with a flash of bright light. The lights in the barn went out. But neither Carolyn or Midge noticed. Their thoughts were on the orange glow over the hill.

"It exploded!" Midge gasped.

Before Carolyn could say anything, a

11

powerful roll of thunder echoed over the countryside.

Midge's shoulders slumped. "Oh, thank goodness," she sighed. "It was just a flash of lightning."

Their relief was short. A figure appeared on the road at the top of the hill. It was Ed Jordan. His hands were cupped to his mouth. He was shouting.

"I can't hear what he's saying," Midge said. She ran out the door onto the driveway in front of the barn.

The lights in the barn flickered. Then they went out for good. Carolyn glanced at the telephone on the wall just inside the door. She had sensed something awful was going to happen at the stable. Now it had. Her first instinct was to telephone the police for help.

"He wants us to call an ambulance," Midge said as she hurried in from the rain. "I couldn't hear everything, but they need help."

Carolyn already had the phone in her

hand. She tapped the numbers and waited. The line was dead. "It's not working," she shouted to Midge who watched the hilltop for further signs of activity. Ed Jordan was not there.

"The lightning must have hit a telephone pole," Midge said. She looked into the Jordan car parked just inside the barn door. The keys were in it. "I'll drive to Watson's Corner. They've got a two-way radio if the phone isn't working." She climbed into the car. "You stay here and keep trying the phone." With that she drove out of the barn and onto the road.

Carolyn tried the phone again. It was useless. She watched her father's car as it neared the top of the hill. Then it stopped. Midge got out. The orange glow was dying down. Midge waved her arms. She was shouting.

Carolyn put her hands to her ears. What she heard chilled her to the bone. "The road is blocked!" she said, repeating Midge's words. A whinny from the back of the stable startled her. She spun around on her heels. Lady was out of her stall. Her rope dragged on the floor.

Carolyn ran to Lady. Obediently, the big horse stopped to wait for her mistress. "Somebody needs help," Carolyn said as she grabbed the rope. There wasn't time to put a riding halter and saddle on Lady. Without thinking about her own safety, Carolyn climbed the stall rails onto Lady's broad back. With the halter rope in one hand and a tight grip on Lady's mane in the other, Carolyn dug her heels into the horse's flanks.

Lady bolted out the door as if stung by a bee. She wheeled at Carolyn's command and headed away from the road. Carolyn was going to ride to Watson's Corner through the backwoods.

Carolyn's long hair flopped over her back as the sturdy Arabian horse galloped across the fields. Her green rain jacket flapped like a flag in the wind. She could barely see through the rain. But she trusted Lady.

They flew across the meadow, barely touching the ground.

Lady leaped over fences. She splashed through a swollen creek. She dodged boulders, bushes, and trees. Her hoofs sliced the soggy meadow turf tossing clumps of dirt into the air. And all the while Carolyn urged Lady on fearlessly.

The horse bounded onto the highway. Watson's Corner was straight ahead. Seconds later, Lady wheeled into the driveway of Watson's Gas Station and Country Store. "Good girl!" Carolyn shouted as she raced inside.

A short while later Carolyn was back in Lady's stall, brushing down her brave horse. Sirens wailed in the distance. Then they faded away and it was quiet again.

Ed Jordan, Harry Carlson, and Midge Sawyer were outside the stable. They were talking with Sheriff Timms. The four entered and walked to Carolyn's side.

"You did a very brave thing," the sheriff said with a broad smile. "Perry is going

*They flew across the meadow, barely
touching the ground.*

to be all right, thanks to you."

"He skidded off the road to avoid a deer," Harry said. "Luckily he got out before the pickup caught fire."

Carolyn's dad said nothing. He was so proud he couldn't speak.

"We've never seen a braver person, and I doubt we'll ever see one," Sheriff Timms said.

"I'm not so sure," Carolyn said as she turned to her horse. "Has anyone seen Lady?"

They all smiled. They knew exactly what she meant.

Roughneck

"Get rid of that horse!"

Badger the Clown was speechless. Roughneck was his pony. It didn't belong to the circus like the others. Roughneck was a part of Badger's circus act. Without him, Badger the Clown wouldn't be a clown anymore. He would be just another circus worker.

"But Mr. Sharpe..."

"No, *buts,* Mr. Badger the Clown," Mr. Sharpe said, mocking Badger's plea. "Get rid of him before tonight's performance or you both go!"

Badger stepped out of Mr. Sharpe's railroad-car office. He paused at the top step.

"Now!" Mr. Sharpe's voice said from inside.

Badger the Clown trudged across the railroad yard where the circus train was parked while the circus was in town. He wore his clown make-up as he always did. On his head was a tight white cap with three bright bunches of orange wool, one on top and one above each ear.

His face was painted white. Fat eyebrows of orange wool that looked like fuzzy caterpillars arched over each eye. His painted-on mouth was a permanent red smile as big as a pretzel. On each cheek was a small blue star, just under the corner of each eye. When asked, he would say they were teardrops that fell from the sky.

Badger's real mouth was very sad as he walked toward the animal tent behind the big top. It was where all the animals were kept when they were not on the train. Badger's baggy pants flopped in the breeze. His loose suspenders drooped. They didn't actually hold up his pants. Buttons inside the waistband did that. But the loose suspenders made it look as if Badger's pants would fall down any minute. The pants were green-checked. Under the suspenders he wore a yellow t-shirt. On his shirt were the words, "Have A Nice Day."

"Hey, Badger! Why the long face?"

Badger turned toward the voice. It came from near the lions' cages. Behind them was Hans, the lion tamer.

"Mr. Sharpe won't let me keep Roughneck," Badger said softly. "He says I can't control him. He says the insurance company won't insure the circus if its ponies are more dangerous than the lions."

Hans scowled. "My cats are wild animals," he said. "Only my skill keeps them from attacking. No circus pony..."

Badger put his hand on his friend's shoulder. "They don't really mean Roughneck is more dangerous than your lions. They only mean that he gets out of control once in a while. They're afraid a spectator might get hurt, I suppose."

Hans calmed down. "Oh, I see," he said. "Well, what are you going to do with him?"

"I don't know," Badger said. He wandered away. Real tears were streaming down his face but Hans didn't notice.

That afternoon the ringmaster announced that Badger the Clown would not appear. He didn't tell the crowd why. A thousand children missed the funny clown's act that day. They didn't know he would never return to the circus.

Badger drove through the countryside in a small rented truck. In the back was Roughneck. The back roads were dark. It had been years since Badger had driven any kind of vehicle. He tried to be careful, but too many things were on his mind. He missed a turn. The truck tumbled off the edge of the road. It rolled over. Roughneck fell out the back. Badger was trapped inside.

The terrified pony ran off. When Roughneck calmed down, he returned to the bend in the road. By that time the truck was gone and so was Badger the Clown.

The next morning Heather Martin sat by the kitchen window eating breakfast. She was bored. She read the back of the cereal box for the third time. She wasn't interested in baseball players but she read about them anyway. It was more interesting than watching her cereal.

Something outside the window caught her eye. "Oh, my gosh! A pony!"

Standing in the garden, knee deep in daisies, was Roughneck. He was sweaty and dirty. He was also very hungry and immediately found the Martins' carrot patch.

Heather jumped from the table. She ran to the kitchen door. "Mom!" she called as she ran outside. "There's a pony in the garden eating your carrots!"

Roughneck looked up as the girl rounded the corner of the house. He had seen thousands and thousands of strangers in his life. He paid no attention but continued to eat the bright green tops off a long row of carrots.

Standing in the garden, knee deep in daisies, was Roughneck.

Heather broke into a wonderful smile. It was the funniest thing she'd ever seen. She let the pony finish the mouthful it was chewing. Then she entered the garden to lead it out. Roughneck obeyed perfectly.

For two weeks Mr. Martin searched for the pony's owner. He placed ads in the local paper. He posted notes on the bulletin boards at the supermarket, the pharmacy, and the town hall. Of course he notified the police. At the end of the second week the police called him at his store. "It looks as if your daughter has a pony," the policeman said. "Of course, if we find out who lost him, he'll have to be returned. But until then, you might as well keep him."

When Heather heard the news she was thrilled. She helped her father convert a corner of the garage into a stall. She helped put in fence posts to make a tiny paddock next to the garage. She carried bales of hay they bought at the feed store. She did everything without being asked. That was because she was happier than she'd ever been in her life. Three weeks after Rough-neck appeared in the garden, Heather tacked a handmade sign over the door leading from his stall to his paddock. "Magic" the sign said. "Because he appeared just like magic," Heather explained whenever she was asked about the name she chose.

That same week a small article in the local paper went unnoticed by the Martins. "Man injured in truck accident released from hospital," the headline said. The story explained that a man had been found trapped under a rented truck that had run off the road one night. It said his name was unknown because he had no papers when he was found. The rental agreement in the truck said only "John Smith."

"John Smith" was really Badger the Clown. He vanished from town before the paper carrying the news about him reached the street.

Magic was a perfect pony. He was very well trained to begin with, of course.

Heather was forever amazed when she would say something out loud such as "I wonder if Magic could learn to canter" and Magic would instantly canter. After a while she began to test him. "Can you trot?" Magic trotted. "Well, I wonder if you know how to pace?" Magic paced. "Can you do the rack?" The rack is an uncommon gait for a pony. Naturally, Magic did the rack. Heather soon learned he could do all the gaits a horse can be taught. They also included the walk and the running walk.

"I wonder who owned you?" Heather said aloud one summer day. She didn't really ever want to find out. If she did, she knew she would have to return Magic. But she couldn't help thinking about who the owner might be. "I'm sure whoever it is misses you very much," she said. The thought began to bother her after a while. She knew how she would feel if she ever lost Magic now that he was hers.

Mrs. Martin was working in her garden. Heather approached her. Heather had just been brushing down Magic. The thought of the previous owner was very heavy on her mind.

"I'm going to find Magic's real owner," Heather said.

Mrs. Martin looked up in surprise. She knew how devoted her daughter was to the pony. She smiled. "That's a very brave thing to do, Heather," she said. She put her garden tools aside and carefully stepped out of the garden. She put her hand on Heather's shoulder. "I'm sure that when you've done all you can, you'll be happier. No matter how it turns out."

Heather nodded.

Heather spent the remaining weeks of summer looking for Magic's owner. She put up notices. She asked other horse owners. She visited stables. She did everything she could think of. Nobody recognized Magic. Nobody had heard of anyone losing a pony. By summer's end, there were simply no more places to check.

Mr. Martin spoke at the dinner table. He

slipped his glasses down on his nose so he could see over them. "I think you can consider Magic your pony now," he said. "You should put your mind to rest."

Heather's mother agreed. "Everybody knows you've tried to find the owner, dear," she said. "Really. Let's all agree once and for all that Magic is yours. My goodness, if you spend the rest of your life wondering, you'll never really enjoy him completely."

It was true. As much as Heather loved Magic, and as much fun as he was to ride and put through his paces, there was always the nagging fear he'd have to go away.

Heather smiled. "I think so too," she said. And that was that. Heather forgot her fear. It was a great relief.

For the next three years Heather and Magic were inseparable. Each day, rain or shine, or freezing cold and snow, Heather tended to her pony. She said good-night to him every night. And when she sat at her desk in her room doing homework, she glanced out the window from time to time at Magic's little paddock or stall door. She let her friends ride him. She groomed him. She devoted her life to him.

In the meantime, Heather herself grew to be a beautiful teen-ager. She no longer had to use a stool or fence rail to climb onto Magic's back. She could step directly into the saddle stirrup. Magic was big enough and strong enough to carry an adult. Carrying the lovely young girl was no effort at all.

On a warm spring day the Martins made a trip to the city. Their small town was far enough away to make the visit an adventure. Heather looked forward to the trip. However, it was the first time she would be away from Magic. That part made her worry.

The Martins visited museums, theaters, and many, many shops. Heather walked happily down the street with her eyes feasting on the tall buildings, the crowded streets, and the crowds of people that seemed to go on forever. "Isn't it wonderful?" she said to her parents who followed a few steps behind. They agreed.

A group of people were gathered in front of a large store. Heather saw them and was immediately interested in what they were doing. Heather pushed forward into the group. The people were laughing at something. Heather began to smile even before she knew what was going on.

In the center of the group stood a man in baggy pants, red suspenders, and a very faded yellow t-shirt that said, "Have A Nice Day." On his head was a tight white cap with three ragged bunches of bright orange wool. Caterpillar-like eyebrows of the same material arched over each eye. A tiny star was painted under each eye. And in the middle of his face was a red make-up smile as big as a pretzel. He was a clown. A street clown. At his feet was a small cardboard box. In it were a few coins. The clown was juggling. He pretended to drop a ball, but it would bounce right back into the whirling circle he juggled. Each time the crowd laughed. And once in a while someone would put a coin into the box.

Heather watched with amazement. Her smile grew into a laugh.

The clown's eyes were on the flying balls. But for a moment his attention went to the sea of faces watching him. Suddenly all the balls fell to the street. He made no effort to stop them or to pick them up. Everyone roared with laughter. It seemed to be the end of his act and, like a puff of smoke, they moved on and were gone. Only Heather and her parents remained.

The clown stared into Heather's eyes. And Heather stared right back.

"Come on, Heather. That's the end of the act," Mr. Martin said. He put a dollar bill into the clown's box.

Heather was transfixed. She and the clown faced one another for only a moment, but somehow it seemed much longer.

"Heather!" Mrs. Martin was already walking away.

Heather turned away from the clown and walked slowly to her mother's side. They continued down the street. At the corner Heather looked over her shoulder. The clown was still watching her.

The rest of the morning was like a trance to Heather. She shopped with her mother, while her dad made a business call. Heather tried on a few things and even bought gifts for her best girl friend. Yet the memory of the clown's face lingered.

That afternoon as Heather and her mother waited on a corner for the traffic light to change, the wail of a siren caught their attention. Many of the pedestrians at the corner didn't even bother to look up as an ambulance sped by. But Heather did. On its side were the words, "St. Mary's Hospital." As it drove away, Heather caught a glimpse of bright orange through the back window. Her heart leaped. "Magic!" she exclaimed in a voice so loud everyone turned. "Something has happened to Magic."

Mrs. Martin was stunned. She took Heather aside as the other people walked by. "Heather? What's wrong?" she asked.

Heather's arms were covered with goosebumps. She was shivering. "I don't know," she said as she put her hand to her forehead. "I had the most awful feeling that something happened to Magic."

Mrs. Martin was concerned. But she didn't know what to do. They were really strangers in the city. Mr. Martin was not due from his meeting for two hours.

Heather looked down the street in the direction of the ambulance. "Can we go to the hospital, Mom?" she asked.

Mrs. Martin gasped. "Are you sick?"

Heather shook her head. "No, Mom, I'm fine. But..."

"What is it?" Mrs. Martin asked.

"Can we go to Saint Mary's Hospital?" Heather asked.

"But, but why?" a confused Mrs. Martin wondered. "I don't even know where it is..."

"Can we go there? Please?" Heather begged.

A policeman gave them directions to the hospital. Mrs. Martin was very puzzled. But she went along. There really seemed to be no other choice.

Something was driving Heather to be bolder than she'd ever been. She went straight to the main desk. "Did your ambulance bring a man here a few minutes ago?" she asked the nurse. "A clown?"

The nurse smiled. "A clown?" she said as if somebody were playing a joke. Then she saw the earnest look on Heather's face. She looked into the computer terminal on her desk. "A man was just admitted," she said. "He collapsed on the street..." She read the information on the screen. "It doesn't say what the problem was. But his name is John Smith. Is that who you're looking for?"

Heather shuddered. "Can we see him?" she said.

Mrs. Martin was astonished. *"Heather!"*

she said.

The nurse explained that the man could not receive visitors. Mrs. Martin called Mr. Martin and he joined them. The family sat for hours in the hospital waiting room. Heather's father and mother were uncertain what they were doing there, but Heather's determination convinced them it was the right thing to do.

Another nurse replaced the first. Much later, she called the Martins over. "The doctor says Mr. Smith can have just one visitor," she said. "It can be only a few minutes. He's a very sick man."

Mr. and Mrs. Martin watched as Heather followed the nurse to the elevator.

Heather entered the hospital room. On a bed lay the man she'd seen on the street. His baggy pants, red suspenders, and faded yellow t-shirt were loosely piled on a chair at the end of the bed. The orange wig lay on a table. But the bright red smile was still painted on. And under each eye was a tiny blue star. He was Badger the Clown.

His eyes were closed. They opened as Heather approached the bed.

The two looked at one another in silence. The man's mouth began to move. "You found Roughneck," he said quietly.

Heather's brow wrinkled. Then it smoothed. She nodded. "I didn't know his real name," she said. "So I named him Magic."

Badger nodded.

"He's a wonderful pony," Heather said. "He's kind and obedient and gentle..."

The clown smiled. "I know," he whispered.

"Are you going to be all right?" Heather asked.

Badger smiled weakly. "I wasn't sure before I met you," he said. "But now I know I'll be fine."

"I'm glad," Heather said. She dug into her purse. "I've got a picture of Magic...I mean Roughneck," she said. "Do you want to see him?"

"Oh, yes," nodded Badger.

Heather held the picture so Badger could see. A real tear dropped from the corner of his eye.

"What's your name?" Badger asked in a very weak voice.

Heather leaned the picture against a glass on the table next to the bed. "Heather," she said.

The clown smiled. "That's a beautiful name," he said. "I've been a clown all my life. I've made thousands of children laugh. But something always troubled me."

Badger's voice grew dim. Heather put her head close so she could hear. "What was it?" she asked.

The clown took her hand. "I never knew any of their names," he said in a whisper. "But now I do."

The nurse entered. "I'm sorry, but it's time to go." She looked at the clown. His eyes were closed. A tiny tear lay atop the blue star under his eye. The nurse took Heather's hand from the clown's.

Heather bit her lip. "What's your name?"

she asked the clown.

The nurse led Heather to the door. "He can't hear you," she said. "He's sleeping."

Heather turned. She went back to the table. She took the picture and placed it in Badger's hands which she gently folded over his chest. She kissed him on the cheek. "Please get better," she said in a brave voice.

Heather visited Badger every day while she and her parents were in the city. When it was time for them to go home, Heather went to say goodbye.

Badger sat up in bed, almost as good as new. "I have a present for you," he said to Heather who stood with her parents at his side. He handed Heather the picture of Roughneck. "Look at the back."

Heather turned the picture over. She read aloud. "For Heather from her friend Badger the Clown. The best circus pony in the world...Roughneck."

"But you can call him Magic," Badger said with a smile.

Heather's eyes opened wide. "Do you mean...?

Badger nodded. "Yes," he said. "He's your pony now."

"But what about you?"

Badger glanced at Mr. Martin. "Your father called the circus. Mr. Sharpe wants me to come back. He wants me to teach new clowns how to make children happy."

Heather threw her arms around Badger. "Oh, Badger!" she said. "Will you come to visit us?"

Badger's smile grew bigger than ever. "Yes!" he said. "Every time the circus visits near you, I'll be back to see you and Roughneck."

And Badger the Clown has been back every year since.

Wildfire

Young's Guest Ranch sometimes touched the clouds. It lay snuggled against the Rocky Mountains of Colorado surrounded by dark evergreen forests. On cool mornings before the sun was very high, gray-white clouds hung over the ranch in giant puffs.

That was what Missy Gordon saw on her first day at the ranch. She was there with her family on a vacation. The Gordons had a log cabin all to themselves. Missy and her sister Lisa shared a big bed in a very little room. Their parents were in the next room.

It was still early. The Gordons had

arrived late the night before. Missy and Lisa were already awake. They were excited. They didn't want to miss a minute of the week they would spend at the ranch.

"Let's get up," Missy whispered to her younger sister.

"O.K.," Lisa whispered back.

The girls had convinced themselves their first mountain vacation would be an adventure. Whispering helped make it seem so.

Both girls quickly dressed in jeans and t-shirts. They slipped sneakers on their feet and tip-toed out the front door.

"Oooh, look!" Missy exclaimed.

The girls viewed the towering mountains with awe. Their own state was as flat as a kitchen counter. The only mountains they'd ever seen were on television or in the movies. These were real.

A ranch house, a barn, and four guest cottages made up the ranch. Four handsome horses trotted nervously in a wooden corral behind the barn. Their quick movement caught the girls' attention.

"Let's go see them," Lisa said.

Missy glanced back at their cabin and then at the horse barn and corral. "O.K.," she said, and they began to run down the sloping hill.

The sisters climbed onto the corral fence. The horses were on the far side in a tight group. The largest, a chestnut mare, tossed her head up and down. The others stood behind her.

"I wonder what's wrong?" Missy said.

"Why do you think something's wrong?" Lisa asked.

"They seem kind of nervous, like something spooked them."

"Maybe it was a rattlesnake," Lisa said dramatically.

"Don't be silly," Missy said.

"I'm not. There *are* rattlesnakes out here, you know. Dad said so."

The horses continued to prance. The chestnut mare broke into a trot. She circled the corral as if trying to get out.

"Well, if it's a rattlesnake, I don't see it..." Missy stopped in mid-sentence. She stared at the mountain above the corral. The clouds had melted. A bright ray of sun burst through the last drifting patches of mist.

High atop a rocky ledge stood a magnificent horse. It was bathed in the spotlight of the early morning sun. An unseen wind blew its mane straight out. Its tail was held as high and proud as its head. It was coal black. Its coat glistened as if it had been rubbed with oil. Its powerful legs were four square on the rocky ledge, as sure as those of a mountain goat.

The stallion tossed its head. The sound of its whinny echoed over and over off the mountainsides. The stallion stood like a king on his throne, the master of everything below.

Missy gasped. The sight and sound of the black stallion took her breath away. She'd never seen such an animal in all her life.

High atop a rocky ledge stood a
magnificent horse.

Goosebumps covered her bare arms and legs. She shivered as if wrapped in a cold wind.

Lisa saw the stallion too. She was speechless.

The horses in the corral trotted round and round. It was clear now what had made them skitterish.

A puff of cloud passed in front of the horse on the mountain. When it cleared, the black stallion was gone.

Missy continued to stare at the empty ledge. At last she spoke. "Oh, Lisa!" she said. "Did you *see* him?"

Lisa nodded silently. She too watched the peak hoping the stallion would return. When it didn't, the girls walked slowly back to their cabin. They turned to face the ledge from time to time, but it remained empty. Even the clouds had faded.

At breakfast in the lodge dining room, the girls told their parents what they had seen.

"I don't think there are any wild horses

around here," Mr. Gordon said. "But I don't know what else it could have been."

"Did I hear you say 'wild horses' ?" a voice asked.

A man stopped at the Gordons' table. "I don't mean to sound nosey," he said. "But I overheard you say something about wild horses, I believe."

The man introduced himself. He was a guest at the ranch like the Gordons. He had come every summer for many years. And he knew about the black stallion.

The man joined the Gordons at their table. He smiled at the girls. "It appears that you two have seen something others have only heard about," he said. "There has been talk for years that a coal black stallion roams the high valleys, but very few have actually seen him. He's called Wildfire. Some even think he's imaginary too..."

"Oh, *no!*" Missy interrupted. "He was real. We saw him."

The man smiled. "I don't doubt for a moment that you did. You've described him exactly as others who say they've seen him."

After breakfast the girls returned to the corral. The horses were as calm as circus ponies waiting to perform. The peaks towering over the ranch were free of clouds. The ledge where Wildfire had appeared was in full light. There was no sign of the stallion.

Each morning for the next five days the girls hurried to the corral as soon as the sun was up. They waited patiently with their eyes on the rocky crag. Each morning they were disappointed. There was no sign of Wildfire or that he would ever appear again.

An unexpected mountain storm kept the girls in their cabin on the next to last day of their vacation. They played word games and read books. Mr. Gordon lit a fire in the fireplace to make the cabin warm and cozy.

Shortly after noon, a knock sounded on the door. Mrs. Gordon answered it. It was the man who had told the story about Wildfire.

"We're leaving today," the man said. "I meant to tell you the other day that if you want to hear more about Wildfire, you should talk to Brandy, the cook."

Missy's and Lisa's eyes lit up. After the man left and the rain had let up, they hurried to the ranch house.

"We'd like to talk to Brandy," Missy said to a tall, thin, elderly man who came to the kitchen door when they knocked.

"Oh, you would, would you?" the man said. He wore a tattered white apron over a pair of faded blue jeans and a red flannel shirt. A pair of scuffed cowboy boots poked out from under the apron that hung nearly to the floor. In one hand he held a potato. In the other was a tiny knife. "Who should I say wants to see him?"

"Missy and Lisa Gordon," Missy said politely. "We're guests and..."

"You're not here to complain about his cooking, now, are you?" the man asked.

"Oh, no!" Lisa said. "It's delicious..."

The man smiled broadly. As quick as a wink, he spun the potato in his hand while quickly working the knife over it so fast the peel fell away in a blur. When he was finished, the potato was skinned and the peel hung to the floor in a single long strand. He winked. "I'm Brandy," he said. "Now, what can I do for you?"

The girls told the story of seeing Wildfire on their first day at the ranch. They explained how they had waited every morning since but never saw him again.

As they spoke, a strange look came over Brandy's face, as if he too could see the daring black stallion on the mountain.

"He's real," Brandy said. "I ought to know. I'm the one who set him free."

The girls were entranced. They sat in the kitchen as Brandy prepared the noon meal that would be served in the main dining room. He spoke to them as he worked.

"You wouldn't think a cowboy would end up being a cook," Brandy said. "Well, neither did I. But that was before I found Wildfire."

"*Found* him?" Missy asked. She was impatient to hear the rest of the story.

Brandy nodded his head. "Uh, huh," he said. "Better than fifteen years ago, if I recollect. And I guess I should." He knocked the handle of the big spoon against his leg. It made a loud thunk. "Wood. Just like this spoon."

The girls stared in amazement.

"I used to be the foreman on the ranch here," Brandy continued. "One day I was down at the barn, just like you two told me you were. It was early in the morning. There was a strangeness in the air. Never felt it before or since, but I knew something was up. Well, I kind of poked around not knowing what I was looking for, and there he was."

"Wildfire?" the girls asked.

"Yup," Brandy said with a far-off look in his blue eyes. "Of course he was smaller then. A lot smaller." He laughed aloud. "You could say he was about the smallest critter I'd ever seen made of horse-flesh."

Missy remembered the giant stallion on the mountain. She couldn't imagine such a beautiful horse had ever been that tiny.

"His momma must have had him just outside the corral," Brandy continued. "Maybe she knew there was something wrong with that little fellow. Maybe that's why she came down from the mountain when it was time..."

"Was his mother a wild horse?" Missy asked excitedly.

Brandy stirred a large pot. He tasted the soup and nodded approval. "Yep. His daddy, too. Those were the days when lots of wild ones roamed up there. Now they're all gone. Except for him."

"What was wrong with him?" Lisa asked. She could scarcely sit still.

"Sickly is the best I can describe it," Brandy said. "Just didn't seem to have the spirit it takes to live free in those mountains. I knew the minute I set eyes on him he'd never make it. Well, I said, what's one more horse around here, more or less? So I kept him."

Missy looked out the window toward the empty mountain ledge. "But if he was so small and sick, what made him well?"

Brandy's face reddened. "Promise you won't tell anyone, at least not until you're on your way home?" he asked.

The girls put their fingers to their mouths. "We promise," they said.

Brandy sat in his chair. He had to move his bad leg with his hand so he could sit. "I suppose it was me," he said sheepishly. "I used to talk to him while he was growing up. I'd tell him he didn't have to be so small and sick. I'd say if you really want to be what you're supposed to be, you'll figure out how to do it. I told him he could be the best stallion in the mountains if he wanted to. But all that talk didn't amount to a hill of beans. Least that's what I thought."

Brandy hit his bad leg with a spoon again. "Then came the day this happened," he said. "I was looking for a couple of horses that got out of the corral. It was dark. My horse fell. Landed smack on a rock with my leg caught between. Well, it was bad. The smell of blood scared off my horse and left me stranded. I was too weak to do much but lie there and wait."

The girls listened as Brandy continued his story.

"What happened then?" Missy asked.

Brandy stepped to the window. He looked up at the empty ledge where the girls had seen Wildfire.

"Well, I'll never know how he knew I was there or how he found me, but that little horse I'd raised from a runt showed up about midnight like he knew exactly what to do. I don't remember much because I'd lost so much blood." Brandy stopped. His voice quivered. He wiped his eye with the end of his tattered apron. "He pulled me clear back to the ranch," he said at last. "Dragged me nearly two miles with his teeth. The doc said I would've been a goner in another hour." Brandy's face brightened.

He hit his leg again for effect. "Well, you can see I'm not gone yet."

"But what about Wildfire?" Missy asked.

"I knew what he was telling me," Brandy said. "He was saying, 'I'm ready to go back to where I came from.' He was letting me know I'd done all I could for him and that he was ready to strike out on his own, the way things were meant to be. So I had the doc take me down to the corral before I went off to learn how to use my new leg." He thunked his leg one more time. "I opened the corral gate and I told him to get back to where he belonged. I told him I never wanted to see him again..."

Both girls gasped. "*Never?* Why?"

Brandy nodded. "If he saw me he might want to come back. He might have doubts about himself. And that wouldn't do either of us any good. I'd done what I could for him and he paid me back with my life. That made us even. The rest is up to him." The old cowboy smiled. "And from what people who've seen him say, Wildfire has done just fine."

"Oh, he *has!*" Missy exclaimed. "I'll never forget him for the rest of my life."

The next day Brandy waved to the Gordons from the kitchen steps as they left Young's Guest Ranch to begin the long ride home. Mr. Gordon slowed the car. An unfamiliar sound echoed through the mountains. "What on earth could that be?" Mrs. Gordon asked.

The girls smiled quietly at one another in the back seat. They knew it was Wildfire.

Smokey

"Are you sure it's a good idea to stay over?"

Mrs. Parker spoke to her daughter Tammy through the open car window. The car was in front of Turpin's barn. Mr. Turpin, the owner, boarded horses.

Tammy slung her rolled up sleeping bag over her shoulder. "Oh, Mom. Don't worry. I'll be just fine. There's a phone in the barn. And, besides, Mr. and Mrs. Turpin will be right over there."

The pretty, dark-eyed girl pointed to the simple house a short distance from the barn. "They're so close they'll probably hear me roll over in my sleep," Tammy said.

Mrs. Parker nodded. "Oh, all right," she said. "But make sure you do get some sleep. If I know you, you'll be up all night with..."

Tammy's smile faded. She turned to the barn. Then she looked back at her mother. "Smokey's just got to get better, Mom," she said.

Mrs. Parker started the car. She knew how important it was for her daughter to stay. She smiled softly and blew Tammy a kiss. "If you need Dad or me, just call," she said.

Tammy was already hurrying toward the barn. "I will," she said. But her attention was already on the horse inside.

Smokey lay on his side. His giant chest heaved. His breathing was slow. His usually bright eyes were dull. Kneeling next to the very sick horse was Dr. Fishbein, the vet. His hands were on the horse's snout.

Tammy walked quietly to Smokey's stall. The three other horses being boarded were in the pasture. The grass was green and juicy. The water in the brook that flowed nearby was cold and clear. All Tammy could think of was how much she wanted her horse to get better so he could be outside with the others.

Dr. Fishbein turned at the sound of Tammy's footsteps. He shook his head slowly from side to side.

Tammy put her hand to her mouth. She wanted to cry.

"He's taken a turn for the worse, Tammy," the vet said. He stood. He was a stout man, not very much bigger than Tammy's older brother, Scott. Most of the hair was gone from the top of his head. A thick moustache and side whiskers made up for the loss. He removed his glasses from his nose and blew on them. "If he makes it through the night he might stand a chance. But right now it doesn't look good."

Tammy choked back the urge to burst into tears. She had known for three days that Smokey was sick. Blood poisoning from a cut on his right leg had invaded his system.

The medicine the vet had given him was not working.

"I don't understand why the infection doesn't clear up," Dr. Fishbein mumbled to himself. "I cleaned the wound. It's even beginning to heal. Yet it's as if the infection were still there."

Tammy had listened to the doctor's explanation before. The open cut on Smokey's right leg had become infected. It was treated immediately. Smokey had seemed to be getting better, when suddenly he became ill again.

Dr. Fishbein packed his medical kit. He handed Tammy a large bottle containing red pills. "Get one of these into him every hour," he said. "You'll have to be his nurse, you know. Call me at any time, Tammy," the vet said as he left the barn. "I'd stay, too, but..."

Tammy interrupted. "I understand, Dr. Fishbein," she said.

Tammy placed her hand on her horse's brow. She smoothed his forelock gently.

"You've *got* to get better, Smokey," she said. "I don't know what I would do without you. You've been my horse since I was little."

The horse's side rose sharply as he sucked in a big breath of air. His huge body shuddered. It was clearly painful even for the animal to breathe.

Tammy lay her head on Smokey's neck. She could feel the blood running hard beneath his dark hide. She loved the way he smelled. For a moment she forgot he was so sick. She remembered long rides on the riding path. She smiled as memories of happy times floated through her mind like sweet dreams.

The sharp click of something striking the side of the barn startled Tammy. She raised her head. The noise was followed by another. It sounded as if a stone had hit the wooden wall with the force of a bullet.

Tammy went to the window. The sun was low in the sky. Evening shadows were growing longer. The paddock outside the barn was still in light, but the woods nearby were dark. The paddock was empty. Mr. Turpin would get the other horses in before dark. For now they continued to graze in the pasture.

A shadow in the woods moved.

"Ben Watson," Tammy said aloud. "What's he doing out there, I wonder?"

As she watched, the shadow raised a stick-like object to its shoulder. It remained there for a moment. At the same instant another loud crack sounded as something hit the barn side.

"He's shooting," Tammy said. She ducked below the window. She waited for another shot, but none came.

Smokey neighed. Tammy forgot at once about Ben Watson and hurried to her horse's side. She opened the bottle of pills and poured one into her open palm. "Here's another pill for the fever, Smokey," she said. She placed her hand by Smokey's mouth. The horse swallowed the pill.

"What's the matter with your horse?"

Tammy jumped up in surprise.

Ben Watson stood in the barn door. In his hand was a rifle. He leaned it against the wall and walked to Smokey's stall. "I heard it was sick or something," he said. "Is it gonna die?"

Tammy's heart leaped. She gasped. "No, he's *not!*" she said sharply.

"Looks like it to me," Ben said.

Tammy knew how sick Smokey looked, too. But she would not admit it to herself. She could not admit it to the likes of Ben. "Well, he's not and you saying so doesn't help."

Ben shrugged his shoulders. "Saying he's not isn't going to help either."

"Who asked you to come in here?" Tammy said.

"Nobody," answered Ben.

"Then why don't you leave?" Tammy demanded.

Ben laughed. "It isn't dark enough yet. Rabbits don't come out until after dark."

Tammy was disgusted. She knew Ben liked to hunt rabbits. But it was upsetting to hear him admit it.

"Hunting is dangerous," Tammy said. "You could hurt somebody someday."

"I'm a good shot," Ben said defensively. "Anyway, it's just a pellet gun. I can get rabbits, but these things won't go through a thin piece of wood so what are you worried about?" He held out a handful of small lead pellets the size of peas.

Smokey coughed and Tammy turned her attention back to him. Ben watched for a few minutes and then ambled out the door.

Tammy spent the rest of the evening bathing Smokey with cool water-soaked rags. It was his fever that was making him so ill. That and the mysterious cause of his infection.

Mr. Turpin stopped by after he'd put the other horses into their stalls for the night. "You just give me and the Missus a holler if you need help, Tammy," he said. "You sure do love that horse, don't you?"

Tammy nodded. She sniffed her runny nose. Tears filled her eyes. It was dark out now.

Tammy spent the rest of the evening bathing Smokey.

Tammy lay on a bed of fresh straw at Smokey's side far into the night. The barn was silent. Outside the occasional call of an owl broke the stillness. The lights in the barn were on, but Tammy felt the darkness outside as if it were cold air. She shivered.

Smokey's fever grew worse. Tammy gave him a red pill every hour just as she was instructed to do. She wondered if the pills or the cooling sponge bath would help.

Tammy didn't want to fall asleep. Her eyes grew heavy. She had to stay awake to be with Smokey no matter what. Silent tears continued to run down her cheeks. "I'm here with you, Smokey," she whispered. She brushed away her tears and stood. She had taken off her boots. She walked on the cool cement floor in her bare feet.

She stepped on something hard. "Ouch!" Tammy lifted her foot. Stuck to her heel was a small, round hard object. She brushed it free. It landed on the cement and rolled to a stop. She picked it up. It was one of

Ben's lead pellets. Tammy made a face. "At least this one won't hurt any rabbits," she said as she tossed the pellet aside.

Suddenly the image of Ben aiming his gun in the woods returned to Tammy like a bad dream. The woods were on the other side of the paddock. The pellets she had heard earlier had struck the barn. When horses were in the paddock, they would be between the woods and the barn. "If Ben aimed at something and missed, the shot could hit one of the horses in the paddock," she said aloud.

Tammy raced back to Smokey's stall. "Smokey!" she cried. "Help me find it. Help me find the pellet...."

The horse didn't answer with either a neigh or a blink of its eyes. Smokey lay in pain, breathing very slowly.

Tammy ran to the phone. "Don't die, Smokey! Please don't die!" she called out as she dialed.

Dr. Fishbein answered in a sleepy voice.

"Dr. Fishbein! Come quick. Come

quick. Please...."

The vet recognized Tammy's voice at once. "I'll be there in five minutes," he said. "Get Mr. Turpin if he's not there already."

Mr. Turpin was there. He stood in the open barn door. His nightshirt hung outside his jeans and his feet were bare. "I heard you scream, Tammy," he said. "What happened? Is it Smokey?" He ran to Tammy who kneeled at Smokey's side.

"Help me find it," Tammy said. She was running her hands over Smokey's smooth hide as if brushing him down after a good ride.

"Find what?" Mr. Turpin said.

"Smokey's been shot, I just know it. That's why he kept getting sicker. There's a pellet in him. We've got to find it and get it out."

Mr. Turpin didn't ask questions. He was uncertain about what Tammy had said, but he too ran his palms over the horse's skin.

Dr. Fishbein entered. "Turpin. What happened?"

The older man didn't stop his search. He turned his head to the doctor. "Tammy thinks Smokey got shot," he said. "She thinks there's a pellet in him somewhere...."

"Lead poisoning!" Dr. Fishbein exclaimed. "Why didn't I see it before?" He dropped to his knees. His hands joined the others as they carefully searched the horse's feverish skin for a wound or a lump.

"I found it!" Tammy was behind Smokey. Her hand was near his tail, close to where it joined his rump. Just above the point of attachment was a smooth, hard bulge no larger than a postage stamp. It was not noticeable to the eye. "It's hot," Tammy said.

The vet opened his case without taking his eye from where Tammy's hand rested. He took out a sharp scalpel and scurried next to Tammy without getting to his feet. He brushed aside her hand. With the skill of years of practice, Dr. Fishbein pierced Smokey's skin and drew the blade across the bulge. A flood of dark blood poured out. The horse whinnied.

"Get my kit," the vet said to Tammy.

Tammy quicky did as the vet said.

"Open it and hand me the green bottle," the vet said.

Tammy's eyes were clear. There were no tears. She couldn't feel sorry for herself or for Smokey now. She obeyed each of the doctor's orders.

Dr. Fishbein cleansed the wound. Then he probed it with a long pair of tweezers. He raised the tweezers. In its jaws was a small round pellet.

"Well I'll be..." Mr. Turpin said.

After the wound was cleaned, Dr. Fishbein sewed it neatly closed. He covered it with a fresh white dressing that Tammy taped in place.

Smokey whinnied. Tammy crawled on her hands and knees over the straw in Smokey's stall to his head. Smokey blinked. His eyes were moist and almost sparkled. His breathing grew steady. Tammy stroked her horse's forehead lovingly. "You're going to be all right now, Smokey," she said. "I just know it."

The vet closed his medical kit. He brushed the straw from his knees and straightened stiffly. Dr. Fishbein smiled at the young girl who still nursed the once gravely ill horse. He and Mr. Turpin stepped outside the barn. The sun was just rising over the paddock. The three other horses began to move eagerly in their stalls to be let out to pasture.

A week later, Smokey joined them. At his side was the young girl who had not given up hope. The young girl who loved her horse more than anything else.

Muffin

Mr. Gringle drove his pony cart through town every day at exactly the same time. He went by the gas station at 7 A.M. At 7:17 he rode by Town Hall. The driver of the 8:30 bus knew he was on schedule if he arrived at the bus stop at the same time as Mr. Gringle. Everyone up and down Main Street relied on Mr. Gringle to keep them on time.

But it wasn't Mr. Gringle who kept such perfect time. It was Muffin. Muffin was an old-fashioned milk-cart pony.

Mr. Gringle bought Muffin on the day he retired from his job as a milkman. He trained Muffin to pull a small cart. Every

*Mr. Gringle rode in the cart
behind Muffin.*

day after that Mr. Gringle rode through town behind Muffin, tracing his old milk route. They were never late and never early, but always on time. That's why Muffin and old Mr. Gringle were Woodbury's unofficial clock.

A newcomer to town saw the little pinto pony and the sleepy old man in the red cart. He mentioned it to Fred, the barber. "It looks like they could ride through town blindfolded," the newcomer said.

Fred nodded with a smile. "You could say that and you'd be right, because Mr. Gringle *is* blind," he said. "And so is Muffin."

Everyone in town knew the story of the blind man and his blind pony.

Valeri Temple was Woodbury's police chief. She stopped her police car at the busiest corner on Main Street. The pony cart stopped next to the police car. "Hi, Mr. Gringle," Valeri said. "Lovely day, isn't it?"

"Good morning, Valeri," Mr. Gringle answered. He tipped his head back as if he were looking at the sky. "It's sunny now," he said, "but it's going to rain this afternoon."

Valeri glanced at the sky. It was clear and blue. There wasn't a cloud in sight. "Are you sure, Mr. Gringle?"

"Sure as rain," he said with a smile. "Just watch Muffin's tail. When it switches like that, a storm is on its way for sure."

Muffin's tail waved back and forth as if it were chasing flies.

"I hope Muffin's wrong," Valeri said. "The dam can't hold much more water."

"She hasn't been wrong in twenty years," Mr. Gringle said. "Well, we've got to be going or we'll be late." He clicked his tongue and Muffin trotted off.

Valeri frowned. The old dam above town hadn't been full in years. But two weeks of rain had raised the water level to the top. More rain would send water spilling over the edge. Valeri was worried. If the dam broke, low areas in town would be flooded.

An hour later clouds appeared out of

nowhere. The boom of thunder echoed in the distance. The air turned cool as a breeze began to blow. Soon it turned into a wind. Dust swirled on the street. Shop owners rolled up their awnings. People at home closed their windows. Dogs and cats trotted past one another without a sideways glance. Even the birds in the trees began to look for shelter. Muffin and Mr. Gringle had known a storm was coming. But everyone else was taken by surprise.

The storm struck with fury. Giant drops of icy rain splattered the dusty streets and turned them black. The wind whipped through the trees scattering leaves like dark snowflakes. The streetlights came on. Cars turned on their headlights. Even though it was still early in the afternoon, it was as dark as night.

Mr. Gringle brushed Muffin's fur coat with a curry comb. Muffin's nose was in her oats bucket. Her tail switched back and forth. "We knew it was coming, didn't we, old girl?" he said over the roar of the wind.

He cocked his head to the side. The fan used to cool the barn had stopped humming. Mr. Gringle knew at once the power was off. He smiled. He and Muffin could find their way in the dark.

Chief Temple's police car was parked at the old dam above town. Its headlights pointed at the dam. It was a simple earth dam that blocked the end of a long valley. Behind it was a lake. Water splashed over the top of the dam. There wasn't room for another drop of water in the lake. But the rain continued to fall in thick sheets.

Chief Temple pulled the hood of her raincoat over her head and walked to the edge of the dam. She looked down the valley. The town lights flickered through the pouring rain. Then they went out. The entire valley turned as dark as the sky. Trouble, she thought. She hurried back to the car. She turned on her two-way radio. "This is the chief. I'm at Parker Dam."

The radio crackled. Ben Byrd's voice came over the loudspeaker in the police car.

"Chief! The electricity is out all over town," he said. "I'm using emergency power for the radio. Any instructions?"

Chief Temple brushed her wet hair back from her face. "Stand by on the radio, Ben. I'll be there in ten minutes."

A loud roar drowned out Chief Temple's voice. The ground beneath the car trembled. She whirled around. The center of the dam was gone. Water poured through a ragged hole and tumbled toward the valley below. "The dam has burst, Ben!" she said into her microphone. "Turn on the siren! Warn as many people as you can. Send Joe in the other car to get the people out of Brookside. I'm on my way there now."

Brookside was the lowest part of the valley. It was where the water would be deepest. It was also where Mr. Gringle lived.

Mr. Gringle listened to the storm. He heard the thunder. And when lightning struck close by, he felt electricity in the air. But a noise that was not thunder troubled him. It was a far-off roar in the direction of the old dam. "I think trouble's coming, Muffin," he said. He led his trusted pony out of her stall and put her back in the traces of the pony cart. "We'd better be ready in case someone needs help." His nimble fingers quickly hitched Muffin's harness. It wasn't the time for their daily ride around town, but they were ready.

Mr. Gringle opened the barn door. He stopped to listen. The roar was gone. But another sound alerted him to the danger. It was the sound of rushing water. He felt the ground with his foot. There was already an inch of water on the ground and it was rising rapidly. He patted Muffin.

"Stay here, girl," Mr. Gringle said. He hurried back into the barn. He knew every nook and cranny by feel. He ran his hands along a beam over his head. A kerosene lantern hung on a hook. He opened the lantern and lit the wick. The warmth of the flame told him it was burning brightly. He hung it on a stick and attached the stick to the seat on the pony cart. The lantern dangled in the air. It would be visible from a long way off. "Now we're ready if anyone needs us," he said, patting Muffin once more.

The rising water already covered the barn floor.

Chief Temple stopped her police car in the middle of the road and poked her head out the window. Black water surrounded it. It was still pouring rain. The small bridge connecting the road to Brookside was gone. The river it went over was now as wide as the whole valley. The chief's face was grim. She spoke on the radio. "The bridge is washed out, Ben," she said. "Anyone in Brookside is trapped and the water is rising fast."

"There's more bad news, Chief," Ben said. "The dam at Clarkson gave way, too. The river's going to rise another twelve feet!"

Chief Temple stared across the black water toward Brookside. The houses there would be completely flooded. If the people didn't get out, their lives would be in danger. "I need a boat, Ben," she said over the radio. "I've got to warn everyone in Brookside to get to high ground."

"I'm trying to locate one," Ben said. He sounded worried.

"Keep trying and let me know the moment you find one," Chief Temple said. "I'm going to blow my siren. It's all I can do. The storm is too noisy for anyone to hear my bull horn." She turned on the siren. Its wail cut through the raging storm.

Muffin stood patiently in the open barn door. Mr. Gringle stood next to her. The lantern hanging from the stick on the seat cast a bright glow over the rising water. The obedient little pony wouldn't move until Mr. Gringle clicked his tongue.

Mr. Gringle cupped his hands to his ears. "Listen, Muffin," he said. "That's the police car siren. Chief Temple is out there somewhere." He turned his head slowly to judge the direction of the sound. Although he couldn't see, his hearing was extra sharp.

"It's coming from near the bridge. Something has happened."

Mr. Gringle climbed into the cart. He took the reins in his hands and clicked his tongue. Muffin stepped out the door into water that was already knee deep. It gurgled noisily around her strong little legs. The wagon rolled into the night. The only light for miles around was the bright lantern dangling above Mr. Gringle's head.

Muffin waded through the water on steady hoofs. She knew every inch of every road in Brookside. There was no danger she would get lost in the storm.

The people in Brookside huddled in their houses. They heard the distant wail of the police car siren, but there was nothing they could do. If they tried to leave their houses with nothing to guide them, they would wander off the road and be swept away.

The current grew stronger over the road. Muffin stumbled, but she didn't fall. She pulled Mr. Gringle's cart straight down the middle of the flooded road. Muffin stopped.

It was a stop she made every day. It didn't matter now if it was dark and stormy. Muffin was on her daily route. That's all that counted.

"Good girl, Muffin," Mr. Gringle said. He reached under the cart seat. He picked up a big brass cowbell he kept there. He shook it soundly. The bell clanged so loud it drowned out the thunder. "That should get their attention."

A window in a nearby house opened. A man stuck his head out. He peered into the darkness across the river that raced over his lawn. "It's Mr. Gringle," he shouted to someone inside the house. A woman joined the man. "Help us, Mr. Gringle," she called. "The radio said we have to get to high ground, but we don't dare leave the house because we can't see the road."

"Come on," Mr. Gringle called back. "Muffin knows the way."

The man and his wife climbed out the window. The water was up to their knees. They struggled toward the cart using the lantern as a beacon.

"Hold onto the back of the cart," Mr. Gringle said. "And don't let go."

The man and woman gripped the cart. Mr. Gringle clicked his tongue. Muffin moved ahead. The man and woman followed safely behind.

Mr. Gringle knew their daily stops as well as Muffin. When they neared the next one, he shook the cowbell again. A flashlight beam danced over the dark water from the window of another house. A boy stuck his head out the window.

The man holding onto the wagon called to the boy. "Get everyone out of the house," he said. "Muffin is leading us to safety."

Three people came out of the house and joined the cart. They held onto the hands of the man and woman. Mr. Gringle clicked his tongue. Muffin pulled the cart to the next stop. When Mrs. Gringle rang his bell, more people came out. They also joined the line. At the next stop a woman with a baby in her arms waded to the cart. She put the baby in the cart and joined hands with the others. Soon a long line of people trailed behind the little pony cart. But there were many more people in Brookside. And the more the rain came down, the more the water rose.

A fire truck was parked next to Chief Temple's car. Its giant searchlights cast an eerie glow over the rushing water. A large tree floated by. The flood was worse than anyone expected. Chief Temple spoke to the fire chief. "It may be too late even if we get a boat down here," she said. "We can't possibly reach all those people in time."

The fire chief studied a map of the town. "I'm afraid you're right," he said. "Their only hope is to reach the high ground here." He put his finger on the map. "But with water covering everything, I don't know how they could ever find it in the dark."

The two chiefs looked across the flood toward Brookside. They were helpless.

The water was up to Muffin's chest. A few inches higher and the cart would turn into a boat. Once that happened, even the sturdy little pony wouldn't be able to keep it on the road. Luckily, all but one house in Brookside was evacuated and the high ground was only a few feet away.

A cheer went up as Muffin climbed out of the flood onto the high ground. The men in the line pushed the cart to safety. Everyone scampered to the highest part of the hill. The mother picked up her baby from the cart. They were all safe.

But nobody was cheering in a small house at the far end of Brookside. Huddled on the roof only inches from the rising water was Bobby Freeman. He shivered in the cold rain. He held tightly to a flashlight. "Help!" he called. His voice was already weak from shouting. It was too faint to be heard over the roaring water and booming thunder. "Help," he cried again. "Please, somebody help me."

Muffin's ears wiggled. To anyone who didn't know her, it looked as if she were shaking off the rain. She whinnied softly.

"What is it, Muffin?" Mr. Gringle asked.
Muffin whinnied again.

Mr. Gringle put his hand on Muffin's
head and felt for her ears. His sensitive
fingers could tell the direction Muffin was
listening. He cupped his hands to his own
ears and turned in that direction. The
rushing water and the voices of the saved
people mixed with the booming thunder.
"Ssshhhh," he said, turning to the people
huddled behind him. They stopped talking.
When the thunder died away, Mr. Gringle
listened again. He heard something. He put
his hand on Muffin's ear. It wiggled. She
heard it too.

"Somebody is missing," Mr. Gringle said.
"Quickly. Someone tell me who it is."

A woman in the crowd turned to the
others. She looked at each face in the light
of Mr. Gringle's lantern. "Oh, my heavens!"
she exclaimed. "Bobby Freeman isn't here!"

Two men stepped forward. "We've got to
find him," one man said.

Mr. Gringle climbed into his cart. "Follow

us," he said. He clicked his tongue and Muffin stepped off the high ground into the dark water.

The men followed the cart just as they had when Muffin and Mr. Gringle rescued them. Muffin moved ahead on steady feet. The lantern bobbed on its stick over the wagon. Its pale glow was the only light on this dark and treacherous night.

The sound of a motorboat caught Chief Temple's attention. She and the fire chief hurried to the washed-out bridge. The boat stopped in the searchlight's sharp beam. "We got here as fast as we could," the man driving the boat shouted. A second man threw a line to the fire chief. He held it firmly as the police chief stepped in. Then he got in. The boat turned toward Brookside. Valeri aimed the boat's light into the darkness. Soon a house appeared.

The boat circled the house. "Empty," Valeri shouted. "Keep moving." The boat turned away. Another house appeared. It was also empty. The rescue boat went up one road and down another. Every house along the way was dark and empty.

"They must have reached safety somehow," the fire chief said over the motor's steady roar.

"I can't imagine how," shouted Valeri.

The boat headed for the high ground.

"There they are," Chief Temple said. She aimed the boat's light at the hill. The group on the high ground gave a cheer.

Chief Temple and the fire chief leaped out of the boat the moment it reached the hill. "Is everyone safe?" she asked.

"No," a woman answered. "Bobby Freeman isn't here. Mr. Gringle and two men are looking for him."

The fire chief turned to Chief Temple. He scratched his head. "Mr. Gringle?" he said with a quizzical look.

The woman in the crowd joined them. "That's how we got here," she said. "Muffin led us."

The two chiefs were astounded as the woman explained how the whole neighborhood had been rescued.

"There's no time to lose," Chief Temple said when she'd heard the story. She and the fire chief got back into the boat. It turned away from the hill and headed toward Bobby Freeman's house.

"There's a light," the fire chief said. He pointed to a small house. The dim light of a flashlight danced in the air over its roof. The boat speeded up. Two men and a boy climbed down from the roof and got into the boat.

"Where's Mr. Gringle?" Chief Temple asked the men.

They shook their heads sadly. "We don't know," one man said.

"Muffin led us here," the other said. "We climbed onto the roof to get Bobby. When we turned around, Muffin, the cart and Mr. Gringle were gone."

The rain had slowed down. The worst of the storm was over. The flood was going down. Lawn furniture, cars and other things began to sprout from the water. But

Brookside was still flooded. The boat continued its search. Bobby and the two men huddled in the back. Chief Temple and the fire chief were at the front. The searchlight poked through the dark. All eyes followed the beam. It stopped on a bright bit of red.

"It's Muffin's cart!" Bobby Freeman cried.

The cart lay on its side against a tree. The stick holding the lantern was gone. And so was everything else. Mr. Gringle and Muffin were nowhere in sight.

Chief Temple turned the light in every direction. Fallen trees, soaked cars and debris were everywhere. But the blind old man and his blind little pony were gone.

The water went down as quickly as it had risen. The narrow road winding through Brookside emerged from the water. Soon the boat was useless. Everyone got out. Nobody said a word. More people were needed to search for Mr. Gringle and Muffin. The group hurried toward the high ground where the others were still waiting. The storm was over. The flood was gone. Only the dark remained.

"Clop, clop, clop..."

Bobby Freeman's face lighted up with a smile as big as a sandwich. "There he is!" he shouted. He ran down the road.

There was Mr. Gringle. Muffin was at his side. Both of them turned their heads toward the shouts and sounds of running feet as the whole group from the boat raced to them.

And from the direction of the high ground, everyone who Mr. Gringle and Muffin had rescued came running and shouting too.

Mr. Gingle smiled. "I don't know what everyone is so worried about," he said as he stroked Muffin's velvet nose. "A big tree floated by Bobby's house and swept us downstream. By the time we untangled ourselves, the flood was going down. I tried to find our cart but it was gone and...well, here we are."

"Hooray for Mr. Gringle and Muffin!" Bobby Freeman shouted. "They saved us all."

The crowd joined in and didn't stop until everyone was back on dry ground and wrapped in fresh dry blankets.

Exactly one year later to the day, the whole town of Woodbury gathered on the lawn in front of the Town Hall. The mayor, Chief Temple, the fire chief and everyone from Brookside had special seats next to the guests of honor. Mr. Gringle and Muffin were in the first row. Mr. Gringle sat in a brand-new red cart with black rubber tires and Muffin stood proudly in its traces.

But the best was yet to come. The mayor made a speech and with a tug of a rope pulled a cloth from a big statue at the corner of the street. It was a bronze statue of Mr. Gringle and Muffin and their cart. Above it on a shiny brass pole where the rescue lantern had hung was a big white-faced clock.

And it's still there keeping perfect time for everyone who passes by.